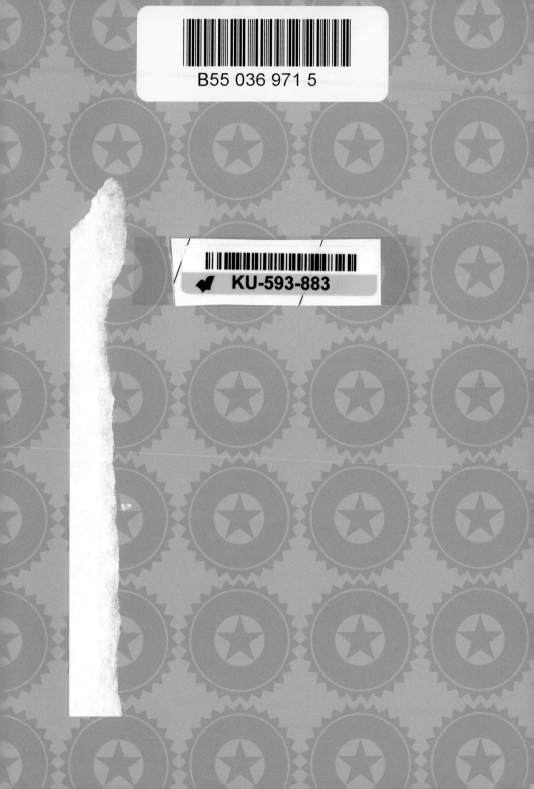

Anansi and the Box of Stories

by Katie Dale and Valentina Bandera

W
FRANKLIN WATTS
LONDON•SYDNEY

Chapter 1

Long ago, the people and the animals lived together as equals. But there were no stories in the world. The Sky God, Nyame, kept them all to himself in a special box. Many travelled to see Nyame to try and buy the story-box, but they all failed.

"The price is too high," they said.

"We'll never get the stories."

Anansi the spider was cunning. He loved stories and he didn't like the word "never".

Anansi went to see Nyame.

"I want to buy your stories," he said.

Nyame laughed. "Even rich princes and powerful lions cannot afford my story-box. There is no way you can pay the price, little spider!"

"What is your price?" asked Anansi.

4

Nyame chuckled. "I want three things:

Onini the python,

Osebo the leopard,

and Mmboro the hornet."

6

Anansi's eight legs trembled with fear. These were

the three deadliest creatures in the jungle!

"Go home, little spider!" Nyame laughed.

Chapter 2

Anansi didn't go home. He went to find Onini –
but Onini found him first.

"Breakfassst time!" the snake hissed.

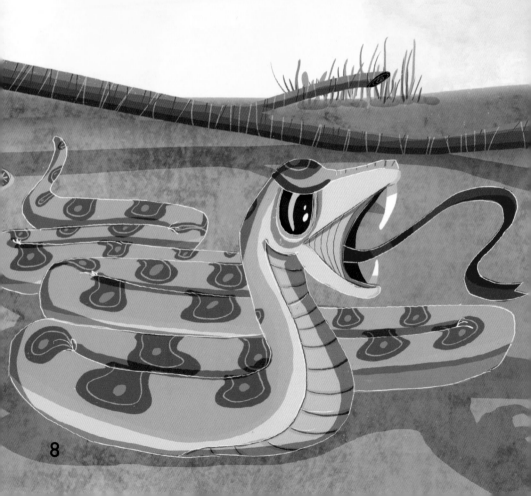

"Please don't eat me!" Anansi cried. He spotted a long branch and had an idea. "Are you really the longest snake in the jungle?"

"Of courssse," Onini hissed.

"But you are not longer than that branch over there." Anansi pointed.

Onini laughed. "I'm MUCH longer!"

"Prove it," Anansi said. "Then you can eat me."

Onini slithered over to the branch and stretched

out beside it. "Well? Am I longer?"

10

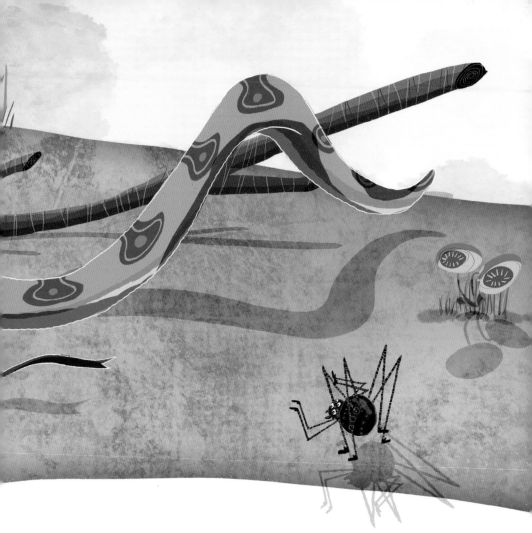

"It's hard to tell," Anansi said, pretending to
measure Onini. "Your body isn't straight. I will tie
you to the branch to see how long you really are."
"Good idea," Onini nodded.

Quick as a flash, Anansi spun a web to hold Onini's body straight.

"I AM longer!" Onini cried. "Now I can eat you!"

Anansi grinned. "No. Now you are trapped!"

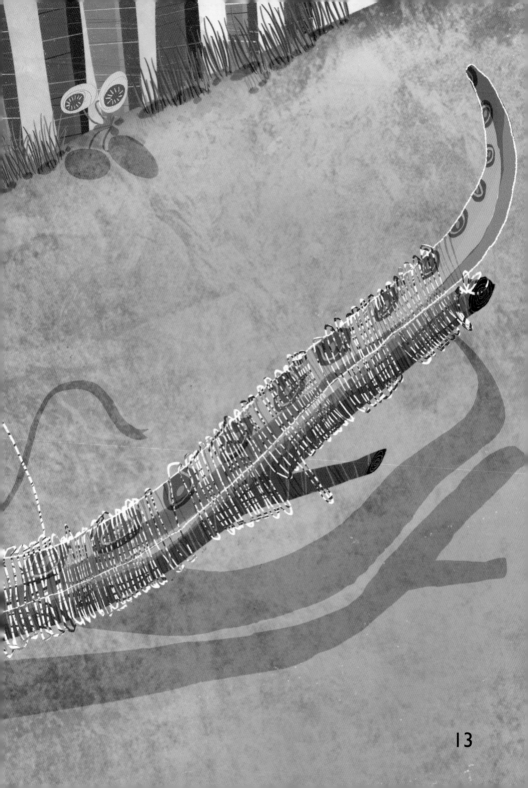

13

Anansi took Onini to Nyame.

"Well done, little spider," Nyame said.

"But you still have to get Osebo the leopard and

Mmboro the hornet – they will not be so easy

to catch."

Chapter 3

Anansi followed Osebo to his cave. As soon as

the leopard was asleep, Anansi started digging.

It was hard work, but by sunrise Anansi had made

a deep pit. He covered it with leaves and branches,

then hid nearby.

Soon Osebo woke up. He yawned, stretched and walked out of his cave towards the pit.

CRASH!

"Help!" cried Osebo from the bottom of the pit.

Anansi scuttled over. "I can help you," he said,

"but you must promise not to eat me."

"I promise!" Osebo said.

"I will tie one end of my web around your tail.

And then I will tie the other end around the tree

so you can climb out," said Anansi.

Osebo nodded.

But as soon as Osebo got out of the pit,

he chased Anansi, his sharp teeth snapping.

Anansi ran round and round the tree as fast as

his eight legs would carry him.

Osebo's tail was still tied to the tree.

As he chased Anansi, he got more and more

tangled until he couldn't move at all.

Anansi smiled, and took him to Nyame.

"Well done, little spider," Nyame said.

"But you still have Mmboro the hornet

to catch, and he won't be so easy."

Chapter 4

Nyame was right. Mmboro's sting was as sharp

as a hot needle and he hardly ever left his nest.

Anansi would have to be even more cunning

to catch him. He thought hard.

Anansi remembered there was one thing

that Mmboro was scared of.

Anansi found a large nut with a hole in it,

and a big leaf. He splashed himself and the leaf

in a watering hole, then hurried to Mmboro's nest.

"Mmboro," Anansi called.

"Who's there?" buzzed Mmboro, crossly. "I'll sting

you for waking me up!"

"I've come to save you," said Anansi.

24

"Save me?" Mmboro laughed. "From who?

I'm not afraid of anyone!"

"The rains have come early!" Anansi said.

He held the dripping leaf over his head like

an umbrella. He tipped it so that water dripped on

to Mmboro's head.

"Oh no!" cried Mmboro. The one thing he feared was water!

"Come, you can shelter from the rain in this nut," said Anansi.

Mmboro quickly flew into Anansi's nut.

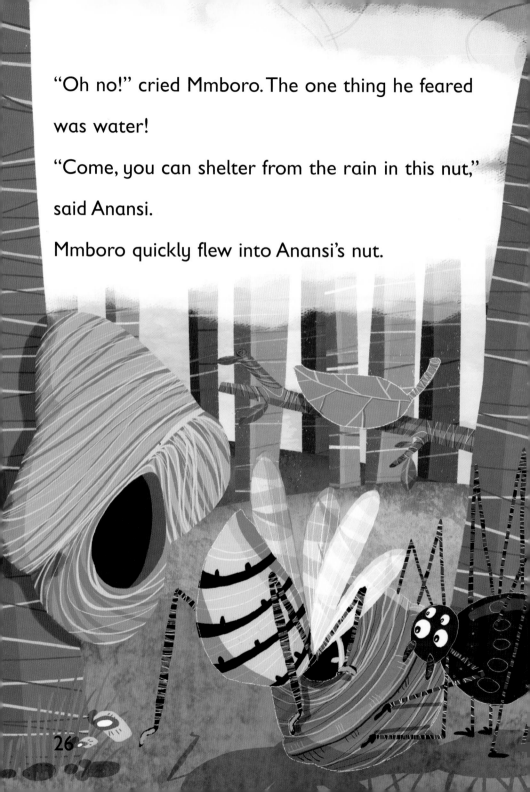

Quick as a flash, Anansi covered the nut with
his sticky thread. He took Mmboro to the Sky God.

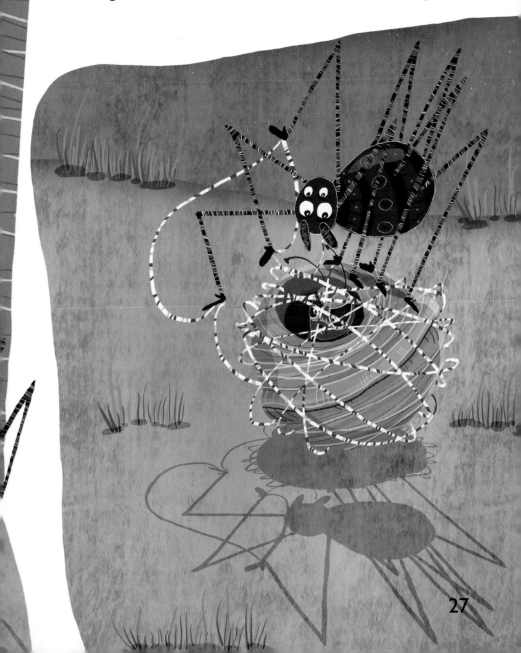

"Well done, little spider," Nyame smiled. He gave
Anansi the box of stories. "You have done what
rich princes and powerful lions could not.
Here is my story-box. It is yours to keep.
Your story is in my story-box, too.
Now everyone will know that even the smallest
animal can achieve the greatest things."

Anansi smiled. And from that day forward, he shared the stories with the whole world – including the story you have just read!

Things to think about

1. What is Anansi like? Think of words to describe him.
2. Do you think Nyame believes that Anansi will be able to catch these animals?
3. Why do you think that Anansi's plans work?
4. Can you think of another story where a weaker animal beats a stronger animal?
5. What do you think the lesson in this story might be?

Write it yourself

One of the themes in this story is that even the smallest animal can do great things. Now try to write your own story about a similar theme.

Plan your story before you begin to write it.
Start off with a story map:
• a beginning to introduce the characters and where your story is set (the setting);
• a problem which the main characters will need to fix in the story;
• an ending where the problems are resolved.

Get writing! Try to use interesting adjectives, such as deadliest, to describe your characters and make your readers understand them.

Notes for parents and carers

Independent reading
This series is designed to provide an opportunity for your child to read independently, for pleasure and enjoyment. These notes are written for you to help your child make the most of this book.

About the book
In this traditional African tale, the trickster character of Anansi the spider manages to outwit the three most dangerous animals in the jungle and release all the stories in the world.

Before reading
Ask your child why they have selected this book. Look at the title and blurb together. What do they think it will be about? Do they think they will like it?

During reading
Encourage your child to read independently. If they get stuck on a word, remind them that they can sound it out in syllable chunks. They can also read on in the sentence and think about what would make sense.

After reading
Support comprehension and help your child think about the messages in the book that go beyond the story, using the questions on the page opposite.
Give your child a chance to respond to the story, asking:
Did you enjoy the story and why?
Who was your favourite character?
What was your favourite part?
What did you expect to happen at the end?

Franklin Watts
First published in Great Britain in 2018
by The Watts Publishing Group

Series Editors: Jackie Hamley and Melanie Palmer
Series Advisors: Dr Sue Bodman and Glen Franklin
Series Designer: Peter Scoulding

A CIP catalogue record for this book is
available from the British Library.

ISBN 978 1 4451 6293 5 (hbk)
ISBN 978 1 4451 6295 9 (pbk)
ISBN 978 1 4451 6294 2 (library ebook)

Printed in China

Franklin Watts
An imprint of
Hachette Children's Group
Part of The Watts Publishing Group
Carmelite House
50 Victoria Embankment
London EC4Y 0DZ

An Hachette UK Company
www.hachette.co.uk

www.franklinwatts.co.uk